The Secret Kitten

By Anne Mallett

Parents' Magazine Press

New York

Copyright © 1972 by Anne Mallett
All rights reserved. Printed in the United States of America
ISBN: Trade 0–8193–0546–4, Library 0–8193–0547–2
Library of Congress Catalog Card Number: 70–174603

THE
SECRET KITTEN

"I think somebody has lost a little kitten."

"Look what we found outside your store, Mr. Pulsaki."

"That's one of mine all right. I just have too many kittens. If you see one you like, you may have it."

"Maybe you had better go home
and ask your mother and father."

"No. It would be too much trouble.
And besides, they make your father sneeze."

"Absolutely not!"

"If I can't give them away, I will have to get rid of them somehow."

"Get rid of them *somehow?*
That sounds sort of scary."

"Are you getting yourself a glass of milk, dear?"

"Where are you going with that box of sand? Please don't spill any of it in the house."

"Have a good night's sleep, children."

"We will."

"Today I want you to pick up your room.
When you are through, I'll come to see what
a good job you have done."

"My! Where has the time gone?
I guess I'd better go in
and start supper."

"She forgot to look at our room.
She forgot to look in our closet!"

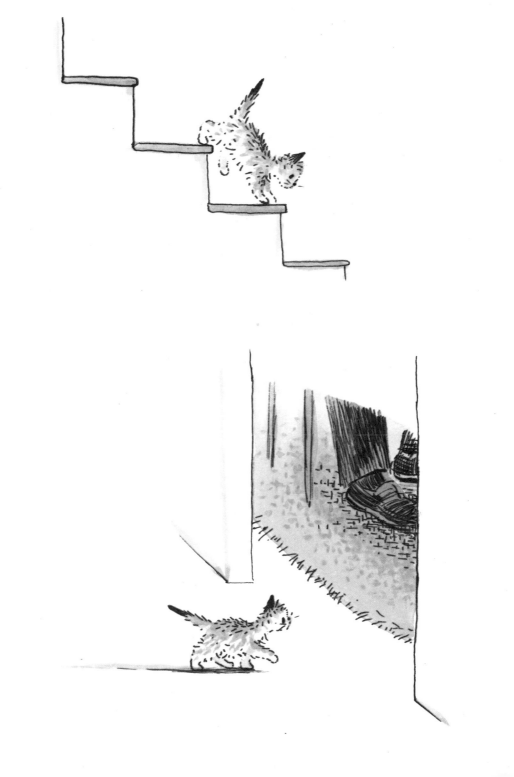

"I got a lot done in the office.
It's been a good day."

"Yes, it has been a good day,
except that I saw a mouse
in the cellar this morning."

"Do you feel like sneezing, Daddy?"

"Of course I don't feel like sneezing."

"Was anything a lot of trouble, Mama?"

"No, nothing was too much trouble.
What funny questions you ask."

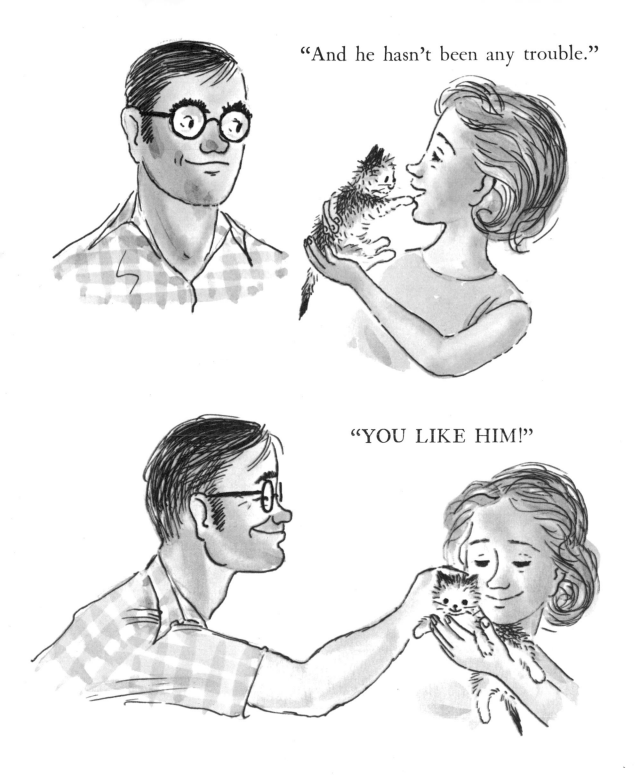

"We can keep him."

"We can keep him."

"We can keep him!"

"We can keep him!"

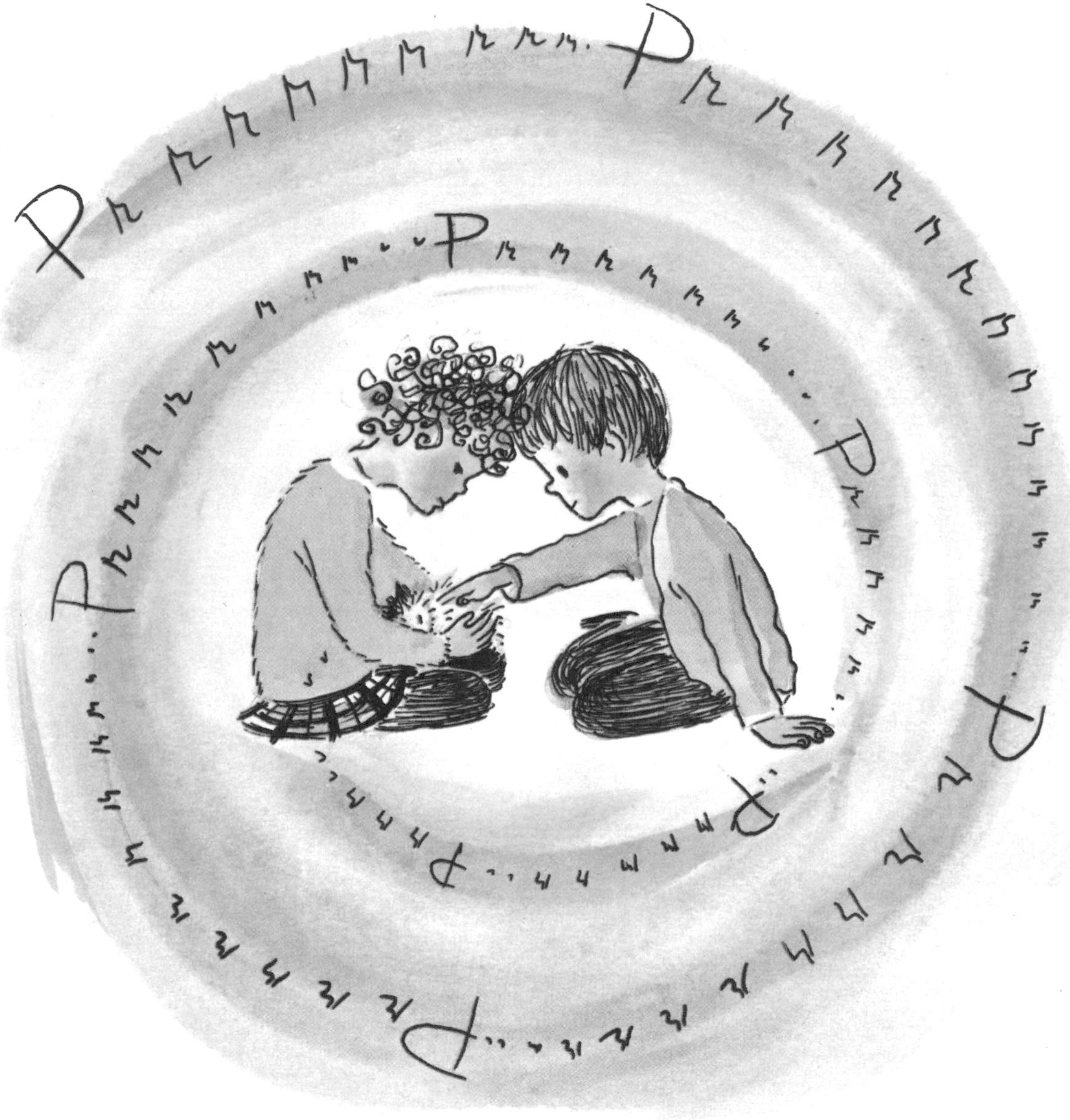